AF228320

THE GEOGRAPHY OF SOUTH ASIA

RACHAEL MORLOCK

PowerKiDS press
New York

Published in 2021 by The Rosen Publishing Group, Inc.
29 East 21st Street, New York, NY 10010

First Edition

Editor: Caitie McAneney
Book Design: Tanya Dellaccio

Photo Credits: Cover Keren Su/Lonely Planet Images/Getty Images; p. 4 saltat007/Shutterstock.com; p. 5 Pyty/Shutterstock.com; p. 7 Feng Wei Photography/Moment/Getty Images; p. 9 (top) Grant Dixon/ Lonely Planet Images/Getty Images; p. 9 (bottom) Sivaraj Mathi Oviyangal/Moment Open/Getty Images; p. 11 Jason_YU/iStock/Getty Images; p. 13 (top) Space Frontiers/Archive Photos/Getty Images; p. 13 (bottom) Rainer Lesniewski/iStock/Getty Images; p. 15 DEA/R. FERRANTE/De Agostini/Getty Images; p. 17 (top) DEA/N. CIRANI/De Agostini/Getty Images; p. 17 (top) Thomas Dutour/Shutterstock.com; p. 19 lipYb Studio/Shutterstock.com; p. 21 hadynyah/E+/Getty Images; p. 23 (top) Rehman Asad/Moment/ Getty Images; p. 23 (bottom) NurPhoto/Getty Images; p. 25 Boy_Anupong/Moment/Getty Images; p. 27 Insights/Universal Images Group/Getty Images; p. 29 Frédéric Soltan/Corbis News/Getty Images.

Cataloging-in-Publication Data
Names: Morlock, Rachael.
Title: The geography of South Asia / Rachael Morlock.
Description: New York : PowerKids Press, 2021. | Series: Explore the world | Includes glossary and index.
Identifiers: ISBN 9781725322127 (pbk.) | ISBN 9781725322141 (library bound) | ISBN 9781725322134 (6 pack) | ISBN 9781725322158 (ebook)
Subjects: LCSH: South Asia–Juvenile literature. | South Asia–Geography–Juvenile literature.
Classification: LCC DS336.9 M667 2021 | DDC 954–dc23

Manufactured in the United States of America

CPSIA Compliance Information: Batch #CSPK20: For Further Information contact Rosen Publishing, New York, New York at 1-800-237-9932

Find us on  

CONTENTS

LAND OF EXTREMES

Eight countries make up South Asia, a region separated from Central Asia by the Himalayas. This vast mountain range is an incredible geographic feature. It's home to the highest peaks in the world and many **diverse** ecosystems. In addition to marking South Asia's northern boundaries, the Himalayas also influence resources and weather patterns throughout the region.

From the giant **expanse** of India to the tiny islands of the Maldives, South Asia is geographically complex and rich with resources. It's a region of extremes, containing the world's highest points above sea level and some of the **densest** populations. Deserts, peaks, and plains can be found across South Asia, and **monsoon** winds, natural disasters, and extreme temperatures shape the lives of its residents.

BECOMING SOUTH ASIA

Massive geological changes created the South Asian region. Also known as the Indian **subcontinent**, the area was once separated from Asia by the Tethys Sea. **Plate tectonics** account for the movement of the Indian subcontinent toward Asia. The two plates collided about 40 million years ago, and the Tethys Sea gradually drained. About 20 million years ago, the Himalayas emerged as the plates continued to crunch together, lifting and folding layers of rock into mountains.

SUBCONTINENT: A LARGE LANDMASS THAT IS GEOGRAPHICALLY SET OFF FROM THE LARGER CONTINENT.

Pakistan, India, Nepal, Bhutan, Bangladesh, Sri Lanka, and the Maldives make up the Indian subcontinent. Afghanistan is also considered part of the South Asian region.

MONSOON: SEASONAL WINDS THAT AFFECT CLIMATE IN THE SOUTHERN AREAS OF ASIA, RESULTING IN WET SPRING AND SUMMER MONTHS AND DRY WINTER MONTHS.

PLATE TECTONICS: THE THEORY THAT EXPLAINS HOW THE CONTINENTS FORMED AND WHY EARTH'S CRUST SHIFTS.

THINK LIKE A GEOGRAPHER

INDIA IS THE LARGEST COUNTRY IN SOUTH ASIA. SPANNING 1,269,212 SQUARE MILES (3,287,244 SQ KM), INDIA TAKES UP MORE SPACE THAN ALL THE OTHER SOUTH ASIAN COUNTRIES PUT TOGETHER.

THE TOP OF THE WORLD

The name Himalaya means "abode of snow" in **Sanskrit**. Snowy Himalayan peaks are among the world's tallest, including Mount Everest on the border of Nepal and Tibet. Everest is the highest point on Earth at 29,035 feet (8,849.9 m). It's still growing since tectonic movements push the Himalayas up a fraction of an inch each year.

The Himalayas cross 1,500 miles (2,414 km) from east to west and measure up to 250 miles (402.3 km) wide in places. The range hosts a variety of ecosystems. Abundant plants and animals **thrive** in alpine, temperate, subtropical, and tropical climates within the Himalayan mountains and foothills. Snow leopards, black bears, yaks, and wild goats live in higher elevations. Elephants and rhinoceroses can be found in the lower ranges.

CLIMBING EVEREST

The summit of Mount Everest is characterized by harsh winds, arctic temperatures, and only a third of the oxygen found at **sea level**. These conditions make it impossible for plants or animals to survive for long. Tenzing Norgay from Nepal and Sir Edmund Hillary from New Zealand were the first people to summit Everest in 1953. Today, hundreds of climbers a year risk their lives to reach the top of the world.

SANSKRIT: AN INDO-EUROPEAN LANGUAGE USED IN ANCIENT INDIA.

SEA LEVEL: THE AVERAGE LEVEL OF THE SEA, WHICH IS USED TO MEASURE ELEVATIONS.

THINK LIKE A GEOGRAPHER

LOCALS IN NEPAL CALL MOUNT EVEREST SAGARMATHA, WHICH TRANSLATES TO "PEAK OF HEAVEN." TIBETANS USE THE NAME CHOMOLUNGMA, MEANING "GODDESS MOTHER OF THE WORLD."

BEYOND THE HIMALAYAS

To the northwest of the Himalayas, the Hindu Kush mountain range cuts through Pakistan and Afghanistan for about 500 miles (804.7 km). The highest point of this range, Tirich Mir, rises to 25,230 feet (7,690 m) in Pakistan. The Hindu Kush contain several important mountain passes for travel within and beyond Asia. The Silk Road, an ancient trade route between China and Europe, historically crossed through the Hindu Kush.

Two mountain ranges, known as the Ghats, dominate the Indian **peninsula**. The Eastern Ghats are a series of hills alongside the eastern coastline of the Bay of Bengal. The Western Ghats run along the Arabian Sea coastline until the two Ghats meet in the south. The Western Ghats are rich in **biodiversity** and older than the Himalayan mountain chain.

LIFE IN THE HINDU KUSH RANGE

High altitudes and low temperatures make it difficult to grow crops around the Hindu Kush range. Cattle and sheep graze seasonally in the high pastures. At lower elevations, farmers use water from mountain rivers and **glaciers** to irrigate, or water, their fields. Rice, walnuts, and fruits like apricots, apples, and mulberries grow near the base of the mountains. Mining in the Hindu Kush mountains can produce silver and lapis lazuli, a deep-blue gem.

PENINSULA: A PIECE OF LAND THAT IS CONNECTED TO A MAINLAND AND IS SURROUNDED ON THREE SIDES BY WATER.

GLACIER: A LARGE BODY OF ICE MOVING SLOWLY DOWN A SLOPE OR VALLEY.

Summer monsoons encourage the growth of a lush, or rich and healthy, tropical landscape on the coastal side of the Western Ghats. They support a rich diversity of plants and animals.

THE RIVERS OF SOUTH ASIA

Three main South Asian rivers and their **tributaries** flow through the Himalayan range. The Indus River **originates** in Tibet and travels northwest through India and into Pakistan. There, it is fed by the snow and glacial meltwater of the Himalayas and Hindu Kush mountains. Then it follows a southern course through Pakistan and empties into the Arabian Sea near the city of Karachi. The Indus River waters the forests, plains, and farms of Pakistan and provides drinking water.

The Ganges and Brahmaputra rivers are also fed by Himalayan snow and glaciers. They begin north of the mountains and travel through deep gorges. The Ganges flows southeast through India, and the Brahmaputra hooks around Tibet and northeastern India. Both rivers pass through Bangladesh into the Bay of Bengal.

THINK LIKE A GEOGRAPHER

THE INDUS RIVER FLOWS FOR 2,000 MILES [3,218.7 KM], MAKING IT ONE OF THE LONGEST RIVERS IN ASIA. ITS FERTILE, OR RICH, VALLEY WAS HOME TO ONE OF HUMANKIND'S LARGEST ANCIENT CIVILIZATIONS.

TRIBUTARY: A SMALL RIVER OR STREAM THAT FLOWS INTO A LARGE BODY OF WATER.

The Brahmaputra River, shown here in Assam, India, is both necessary and challenging to the people living on its shores. Frequent flooding around the river can be highly destructive.

BAY OF BENGAL

The Ganges and Brahmaputra Rivers meet in central Bangladesh, and then the rivers branch out again. Smaller channels flow into the Ganges-Brahmaputra **delta** along the Bay of Bengal. As the world's largest delta, the area covers 220 miles (354 km) in India and Bangladesh. The main river travels further through Bangladesh, eventually ending in the salt water of the Bay of Bengal.

Indian rivers from the west—including the Krishna, Godavari, Mahanadi, and Kaveri—also empty into the Bay of Bengal. This is the largest bay in the world and represents the northeastern portion of the Indian Ocean. India, Bangladesh, Sri Lanka, and the Malay Peninsula surround the bay. Monsoon winds and heavy rain affect the Bay of Bengal every year. They can cause deadly **cyclones** in the spring and fall.

THE SUNDARBANS

The wetlands of the Ganges-Brahmaputra delta are known as the Sundarbans. **Mangrove** forests, palm trees, and swamp grasses grow in the area. An abundance of aquatic birds, fish, and animals thrive in shallow delta waters. Wild boars, macaques, monitor lizards, crocodiles, pythons, and Bengal tigers also roam the Sundarbans. The mineral-rich soil of the delta supports the growth of rice and tea, while the waters are an important source for the fish and seafood trade.

CYCLONE: A TROPICAL STORM WITH HIGH WINDS AND HEAVY RAINS.

MANGROVE: A TROPICAL TREE WITH EXPOSED, TANGLED ROOTS THAT GROWS WELL IN MARSHES OR SHALLOW WATERS.

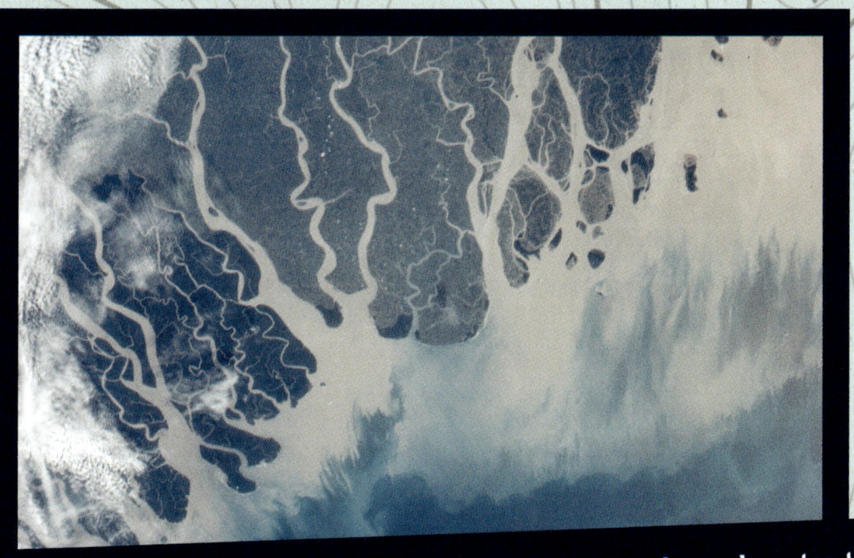

This aerial image of Bangladesh shows how river channels enter the Bay of Bengal through the Ganges-Brahmaputra delta. The delta makes up most of the land in Bangladesh.

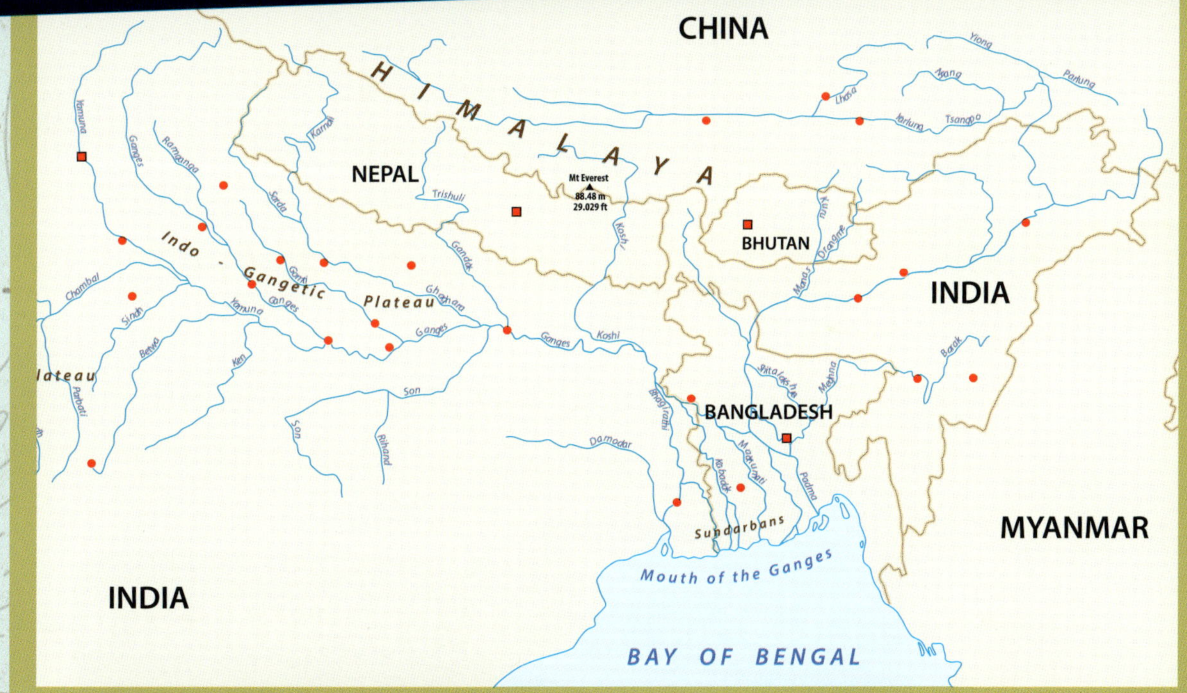

THINK LIKE A GEOGRAPHER

NEAR THE MOUTH OF A RIVER, THE SLOW FLOW OF SMALL WATER CHANNELS ALLOWS SEDIMENT TO BUILD UP. THIS SEDIMENT FORMS A DELTA BY EXTENDING THE LAND INTO THE NEIGHBORING BODY OF WATER.

THE INDO-GANGETIC PLAIN

Just as the Ganges-Brahmaputra delta is filled with mineral-rich soil, so is the region at the foot of the Himalayas through Pakistan, India, Nepal, and Bangladesh. This fertile stretch of land is called the Indo-Gangetic Plain, named for the Indus and Ganges rivers. The plain was originally created from the sedimentary materials of the Tethys Sea.

Since its formation, this bed of rich soil has been growing with sediment deposits from the Himalayas. These are carried through the three main South Asian river basins. The Indus, Ganges, and Brahmaputra **river systems** deposit soil, silt, sand, and gravel along their shores as they flow and flood. The soil is called alluvium, and it's up to 6,000 feet (1,828.8 m) deep in some areas of the Indo-Gangetic Plain.

THINK LIKE A GEOGRAPHER

A RIVER BASIN IS AN AREA OF LAND, OFTEN QUITE LARGE, THAT'S DRAINED BY A RIVER AND ITS TRIBUTARIES. THE PART OF THE GANGES RIVER BASIN THAT'S LOCATED IN INDIA IS HOME TO ABOUT 400 MILLION PEOPLE.

RIVER SYSTEM: ONE MAIN RIVER AND ITS TRIBUTARIES.

SOUTH ASIA'S BREADBASKET

Fertile alluvial soils make the Indo-Gangetic Plain the most heavily farmed zone in South Asia. The plain is sometimes called South Asia's breadbasket because rice, wheat, and grains grow well in the area's rich soil. Sugarcane, maize, cotton, and other crops are also successfully harvested there. In addition to being central for farming, the Indo-Gangetic Plain also contains the densest populations in the region. About one-seventh of the world's population lives in the Indo-Gangetic Plain.

In Baltisan, Pakistan, alluvium is carried in streams down the steep Karakoram mountains to farms below. The triangle-shaped patches of sediment left behind are called alluvial fans.

EXPLORING PLATEAUS AND DESERTS

The Thar Desert is a part of the Indo-Gangetic Plain that lies mainly in northwestern India and reaches into eastern Pakistan. It's the world's most densely populated desert and spans 77,000 square miles (199,429.1 sq km) of sandy plains, dunes, and sparse plant growth. Temperatures rise in May and June, hitting up to 122°F (50°C). This is also a time for seasonal dust storms. Other South Asian deserts are mainly found in Afghanistan and Pakistan.

Further south in India, the arid, or very dry, Deccan **Plateau** lies between the Arabian Sea and Bay of Bengal. The Eastern Ghats and Western Ghats enclose this vast plateau, which is one of the oldest features of the subcontinent. High population density in the Deccan Plateau is a threat to the natural environment there.

THINK LIKE A GEOGRAPHER

THE DECCAN PLATEAU IS MOSTLY ARID BECAUSE THE GHATS PROTECT IT FROM MONSOON WINDS AND RAIN. IT LIES 1,000 TO 2,500 FEET (304.8 TO 762 M) ABOVE SEA LEVEL.

PLATEAU: A BROAD, FLAT, HIGH PIECE OF LAND.

Nomads make camp in the Registan Desert of Afghanistan. In winter months, they bring their sheep, goats, and camels to graze around the nearby Helmand and Arghandab rivers.

KALI GANDAKI GORGE

The Kali Gandaki **Gorge** in Nepal may be the deepest gorge in the world. The highest mountain peaks in the Himalayas sit on either side of the gorge—Annapurna to the east and Dhaulagiri to the west. This gorge, nestled between towering mountains, is 3 miles (4.8 km) long and 1.5 miles (2.4 km) wide. The Kali Gandaki River travels along the gorge and beyond. For centuries, the gorge has served as a trade route between India and Tibet.

GORGE: A STEEP, NARROW PASSAGE THROUGH LAND.

A TRIP TO TROPICAL ISLANDS

Sri Lanka and the Maldives are South Asian island nations. Sri Lanka, formerly called Ceylon, is located in the Indian Ocean near the southeastern tip of India. Its coast of sandy beaches and rocky cliffs encircles a plain that makes up most of the island's area. The plain surrounds the central highlands of the island, which are composed of plateaus and mountains at high elevations.

The Maldives are an **archipelago** in the Indian Ocean, southwest of the Indian peninsula. This 510-mile (820.8 km) chain of 1,200 small islands is made of the tips of underwater, ancient volcanic mountains. About 200 of these islands are inhabited, or home to people. The islands are clustered together into small, ring-shaped groups called atolls. White sand beaches, coral reefs, and lagoons attract visitors to their shores.

ARCHIPELAGO: A GROUP OF ISLANDS.

INDIA'S ISLANDS

The Andaman and Nicobar Islands are Indian islands near the southern coastline of Myanmar. The Andaman Islands are an archipelago of about 300 islands. The Nicobar Islands to the south include about 19 islands. These islands form an arc. The Bay of Bengal is west of the arc, and the Andaman Sea is to the east. Features of the tropical islands include beaches, forests, high peaks, and an abundance of coconut trees. Some indigenous, or native, groups live on these islands, and avoid contact with the larger world.

The World's End **escarpment** drops 4,000 feet [1,219.2 m] from the edge of the Horton Plains plateau. The escarpment is located in Sri Lanka's central highlands.

THINK LIKE A GEOGRAPHER

THE MALDIVES REPRESENT THE SMALLEST AND LOWEST COUNTRY IN SOUTH ASIA. SOME ISLETS, OR SMALL ISLANDS, BARELY RISE ABOVE SEA LEVEL, AND THE ISLANDS HAVE AN AVERAGE ELEVATION OF 4 FEET [1.2 M].

CITIES OF SOUTH ASIA

In this densely populated part of the world, cities are huge, busy, and crowded. Many large Indian cities are located in the Indo-Gangetic Plain near the Ganges River. Over 29 million people live in New Delhi, India's capital city. Mumbai is the second largest Indian city with over 20 million residents. It's located on India's western coast, near the Arabian Sea.

Other important South Asian cities are scattered throughout the region. Dhaka is the busy capital of Bangladesh, and it has a population of over 20 million. Kabul is the capital city of Afghanistan with about 4 million people. Over 1 million people live in Islamabad, the capital of Pakistan. Kathmandu, Nepal, is another capital city with more than 1 million residents.

THE CAPITAL OF BHUTAN

Thimphu, Bhutan, is the least populated capital city in South Asia. The capital is the largest city in Bhutan and the home of about 100,000 people, including the country's royal family. Thimphu is nestled into a valley in the eastern Himalayas along the Raidak River. The Raidak is a tributary of the Brahmaputra River that's fed by Himalayan snow and glaciers. Farmers use a technique called **terrace farming**, growing rice, corn, and maize right alongside the city of Thimphu.

TERRACE FARMING: A METHOD OF FARMING WHERE FLAT STEPS ARE BUILT INTO THE SIDE OF A HILL OR MOUNTAIN TO CONTROL THE FLOW OF WATER.

IN ADDITION TO BEING THE LARGEST COUNTRY IN SOUTH ASIA, INDIA IS ALSO THE MOST DENSELY POPULATED. ABOUT 1.3 BILLION PEOPLE LIVE IN INDIA, MAKING IT THE SECOND-MOST POPULATED COUNTRY IN THE WORLD.

With so many people and vehicles crowding the streets of New Delhi, poor air quality and pollution are critical problems.

ENVIRONMENT AND CLIMATE

From north to south, the climate of South Asia changes dramatically, and so do its **biomes**. The northern mountain highlands are cold and snowy. Around the foothills and valleys of the Himalayas in Nepal, Bhutan, and India, a **humid** subtropical zone encourages a lush forest biome that supports diverse plant and animal life. A desert zone stretches across Afghanistan, Pakistan, and Northwestern India. The semiarid zone of central India and the Deccan Plateau is characterized by high temperatures and fairly low rainfall. Finally, a tropical wet zone with high temperatures and heavy rainfall encompasses Bangladesh, coastal stretches of India, and the southern islands.

Yearly monsoons have an enormous impact on life in South Asia, especially in the tropical wet zone. **Earthquakes** regularly threaten the mountain ranges. Meanwhile, **typhoons** and **tsunamis** are a threat to populations along the coast.

NATURAL DISASTERS

Residents of South Asia have witnessed some of the worst natural disasters in recent history. Floods, **droughts**, and heat waves occur frequently in the region. In 2004, a tsunami killed more than 230,000 people, including those living in South Asian countries of India, Bangladesh, Sri Lanka, and the Maldives. A deadly earthquake shook Nepal in 2015, **displacing** 2.8 million people. Cyclones, or typhoons, have been especially harmful to people and farmlands in Bangladesh. As climate change causes extreme weather, South Asia can expect more frequent and destructive natural disasters.

From June to September, monsoons bring much-needed moisture to dry land, but they can also flood rivers, cities, and towns. The rains are caused by southwest winds that carry moisture from the ocean into the subcontinent.

TSUNAMI: A LARGE OCEAN WAVE THAT IS CAUSED BY AN EARTHQUAKE ALONG THE FLOOR OF THE OCEAN.

TYPHOON: A SEVERE TROPICAL STORM CHARACTERIZED BY HIGH WINDS THAT ORIGINATES IN THE INDIAN OCEAN OR WESTERN PACIFIC OCEAN.

THINK LIKE A GEOGRAPHER

EARTHQUAKES OCCUR ABOUT FOUR TIMES A YEAR IN THE HINDU KUSH RANGE WHEN PRESSURE IS RELEASED BETWEEN THE INDIAN SUBCONTINENT AND EURASIAN PLATE. ONE SOLUTION IS TO BUILD HOMES AND STRUCTURES THAT CAN WITHSTAND THE FORCE OF EARTHQUAKES.

EARTHQUAKE: A SHAKING OF EARTH'S SURFACE CAUSED BY THE MOVEMENT OF LARGE PIECES OF LAND CALLED PLATES THAT RUN INTO EACH OTHER.

RICH IN RESOURCES

Natural resources in South Asia include alluvial soil, water, forests, and minerals. About 42 percent of South Asian land is used for agriculture. Across this region, farmers grow grains like barley, corn, and wheat. Wet zones allow rice, tea, and tropical fruits to grow. Some dry zones are suited to growing dates, figs, apricots, cherries, olives, and grapes.

Freshwater from snow, glaciers, and rivers supplies drinking water to large populations. Water sources are also used for fishing, irrigation, and transportation. In Bhutan, Nepal, and parts of India, hydropower—electricity from moving water—is becoming a popular energy source.

Forests are another chief resource, containing trees and plants such as sal, teak, bamboo, and sandalwood. Highland forests are made up of pines and firs. Unfortunately, **deforestation** has caused soil erosion, flooding, landslides, and the loss of natural habitats in both areas.

MINING IN SOUTH ASIA

Mineral resources boost the South Asian economy. Coal, mica, manganese, and iron ore are important **exports** for India. Natural gas is another plentiful resource in India, Pakistan, and Bangladesh. India and Sri Lanka are well known for their gemstones, including sapphires and rubies. Minerals like gypsum, chromium, bauxite, and copper are mined throughout the region. However, minerals are non-renewable resources, which means they can run out. Many South Asian countries are also exploring the potential of wind, solar, and hydropower as **renewable resources**.

THINK LIKE A GEOGRAPHER

RICE IS A STAPLE CROP IN SOUTH ASIA. IT'S THE MAIN FOOD SOURCE FOR ABOUT 135 MILLION PEOPLE IN BANGLADESH.

Rice grows on a terraced hillside in Nepal. Terraces are designed to flood and spill over into the next step. They keep in the water and nutrients needed for rice to grow.

ADAPTING TO THE ENVIRONMENT

Since ancient times, people have made the most of South Asia's geographical features and environment. Natural mountain passes have become important trade routes. Mountain herders have found a source of warm woolen clothing from sheep and transportation from the yaks who graze in the area. In places with frequent flooding, farmers have perfected farming crops that grow well in wet environments, like rice.

New technologies and practices are still being developed to make life in the region safer and easier. Air conditioning systems combat heat waves, and salt is removed from drinking water through a process called desalinization, or desalination. However, harsh environments and changing climates still make life difficult. Earthquakes, flooding, and droughts drive people from their homes. Population growth as a result of **migration** can stretch and dangerously reduce resources.

THINK LIKE A GEOGRAPHER

PEOPLE IN BANGLADESH HAVE ADAPTED TO THEIR COUNTRY'S WET ENVIRONMENT BY CREATING FLOATING GARDENS ON FLOODED LANDS OR PONDS. THEY ALSO BUILD WALLS AND ARTIFICIAL ISLANDS TO PROTECT THEIR HOMES FROM WATER.

MIGRATION: MOVEMENT FROM ONE REGION TO ANOTHER.

GLOBAL WARMING: THE WARMING OF THE EARTH'S ATMOSPHERE AS A RESULT OF THE HUMAN USE OF FOSSIL FUELS.

The Khyber Pass is a natural opening in the Hindu Kush mountains. The pass has evolved over centuries as an important trade route between Afghanistan and Pakistan. Today, travelers use vehicles and camels to cross the pass.

CULTURAL LANDSCAPES

South Asia is an extraordinarily large and varied region. Its 2.4 million square miles (6.2 million sq km) are marked by plentiful landforms, waterways, and weather patterns. The region is full of stark contrasts. Comparisons—such as those between temperatures in Mt. Everest and the Maldives, or rainfall in the Thar Desert and the river valleys of Bangladesh—reveal how geographically diverse the region can be.

Almost 2 billion people live in South Asia, and their lives, agriculture, and industries have been defined by the natural geography of the land. Likewise, human activities have affected the region. Social and geological history, seasonal and climatic changes, and human migrations and activities are all strong forces that will continue to shape the **cultural landscapes** of South Asia.

SAARC

The South Asian Association for Regional Cooperation [SAARC] was formed in 1985 and includes all eight countries of South Asia. As neighbors, the countries of the SAARC recognize that they share more than borders with each other. Their countries are connected by geography, climate, culture, and resources. The SAARC countries are most successful when they form economic and political connections with each other, share technologies and ideas, and work together to improve life in South Asia.

THE WESTERN THAR DESERT EXPERIENCES AN AVERAGE OF 4 INCHES (10.2 CM) OF RAINFALL PER YEAR. IN CONTRAST, THE MOST RAINFALL IN SOUTH ASIA IS USUALLY RECORDED IN CHERRAPUNJI, INDIA, WHICH AVERAGES ABOUT 450 INCHES (1,143 CM) OF RAINFALL A YEAR.

The Himalayas and the Indus River, shown here in India, are major geographical features that supply essential resources for the South Asian region.

GLOSSARY

biodiversity: The number of different types of living things that are found in a certain place on Earth.

biome: A natural community of plants and animals, such as a forest or desert.

delta: A pile of earth and sand that collects at the mouth of a river.

dense: Closely packed together.

displace: To remove someone or something.

diverse: Different or varied.

drought: A long period of very dry weather.

expanse: A wide space, area, or stretch.

export: A good sold to another country.

humid: Containing moisture.

industrial: Having to do with systems of work.

nomad: A person who moves from place to place.

originate: To come into existence.

pilgrimage: A journey to a sacred place.

thrive: To grow strong, or to do well.

FOR MORE INFORMATION

BOOKS

Bolt Simons, Lisa M. *Mount Everest*. Lake Elmo, MN: Focus Readers, 2018.

Chapman, Simon. *Himalayas: Bottom to Top*. London, UK: Harper Collins Publishers Limited, 2017.

Ganeri, Anita. *Journey Through India*. London, UK: Franklin Watts, 2016.

WEBSITES

Bhutan Facts for Kids

www.kids-world-travel-guide.com/bhutan-facts.html
Learn more about the geography of Bhutan through the text and photographs on this site.

Monsoon

kids.kiddle.co/Monsoon
If you're curious about monsoons, this website might answer some of your questions about how they work and why they matter in South Asia.

Nepal

kids.nationalgeographic.com/explore/countries/nepal/
This overview introduces you to the people, animals, and geography of Nepal.

INDEX